This fun phonics reader

belongs to

D1042416

Contents

Cover illustration by Becky Cole

A catalogue record for this book is available from the British Library

Published by Ladybird Books Ltd
80 Strand London WC2R 0RL
A Penguin Company

8 10 9

© LADYBIRD BOOKS LTD MM

Printed in China

splat cat

by Alison Guthrie
illustrated by Becky Cole

introducing the short **a** sound,
as in cat

My cat Nat is a fat cat.

He likes
a pat

and to sit
and chat.

My cat Nat is a flat cat.

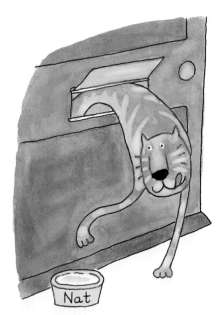

I say to my cat,
"Don't do that!"

That's my cat Nat,

and I like him like that.

Jam-packed

by Richard Dungworth
illustrated by Sami Sweeten

84N GER

more on the short **a** sound,
as in v**a**n

I sat in the van with
Dad and Gran.

I had the map.
The cats sat on my lap.

Mum and Max were
in the back

with Max's pet rat,

Sam the dog and baby Jack.

"Ten in a van – that's not bad!" said Dad.

"But what about the bags?"

Ben's ten hens

by Mandy Ross
illustrated by Leonie Shearing

introducing the short **e** sound,
as in h**e**n

Ken had a hen and

Jen had
a hen.

Len had
a hen

but Ben had ten hens!

When Ken and Jen and Len
met Ben...

how many hens did they all have then?

Posh pets

by Richard Dungworth
illustrated by Brigitte McDonald

more on the short **e** sound,
as in p**e**t

Would you let your pet get a TV set?

When Rex met Meg

Would you let your pet
get a big red jet?

Would you let your pet
have tea in bed?

Would you let your pet see the very best vet?

Dr. PETSKI

· Notice ·
VET'S FEE
£1000

RECEPTIO

You bet!

Pigs in Wigs

by Mandy Ross
illustrated by Rob Hefferan

introducing the short **i** sound,
as in p**i**g

A big pig.

A little pig.

A big wig.

A little wig.

A big pig in a little wig

and a little pig in a big wig.

No, no, no!

A big pig in a big wig

and a little pig in
a little wig.

Yes, yes, yes!

phonics

Learn to read with Ladybird

phonics is one strand of Ladybird's **Learn to Read** range. It can be used alongside any other reading programme, and is an ideal way to support the reading work that your child is doing, or about to do, in school.

This chart will help you to pick the right book for your child from Ladybird's three main **Learn to Read** series.

Age	Stage	Phonics	Read with Ladybird	Read it yourself
4-5 years	Starter reader	Books 1-3	Books 1-3	Level 1
5-6 years	Developing reader	Books 2-9	Books 4-8	Level 2-3
6-7 years	Improving reader	Books 10-12	Books 9-16	Level 3-4
7-8 years	Confident reader		Books 17-20	Level 4

Ladybird has been a leading publisher of reading programmes for the last fifty years. **phonics** combines this experience with the latest research to provide a rapid route to reading success.

● Some common words, such as 'would', 'what' and even 'the', can't be read by sounding out. Help your child practise recognising words like these so that he can read them on sight, as whole words.

Phonic fun

Write simple three-letter words on cards. Cut off the first letter of each. Help your child pair up initial letters with endings to make and read as many words as he can. Then cut the endings into separate letters, and play the game again.

s e t   b a t

Books in the phonics series

Book 1 Alphapets
Introduces the most common sound made by each letter, and the capital and small letter shapes.

Book 2 Splat cat
Simple words including the short vowel sounds **a** **e** and **i** as in cat, hen and pig.

Book 3 Hot fox
Simple words including the short vowel sounds **o** and **u** ; simple words including **ch** **sh** or **th**.

Book 4 Stunt Duck
Simple words including the common consonant combinations **ck** **ll** **ss** and **ng**.

Book 5 Sheriff Showoff
More words including common consonant blends: **ff** **st** **mp** **lp** **nch** **nd** and **fl**.

Book 6 Frank's frock
More words including common consonant blends: **fr** **nk** **cl** **tr** **gr** and **nt**.

Match the sounds gam

36 self-checking phonic gamecards. Great fun, and the ide way to practise the spellings and s introduced in the phonics stor

Book 7 The ace space race
Introduces the **magic e** spelling pattern of long
vowel sounds as in name, bike, mole and rude.

Book 8 Joe's showboat
Long vowel sounds: **ai** as in rain and day; **ee** as
in sheep and dream; and **oa** as in boat and show.

Book 9 Baboon on the moon
More long vowel sounds and their spellings: **ie**
as in sky and high and **oo** as in blue and few.

Book 10 The royal boil
Introduces several more complex vowel sounds –
oy **ow** and **ar** – in their various spellings.

Book 11 The hairy bear scare
More words with more complex vowel sounds –
air **or** and **er** – in their various spellings.

Book 12 Bella's bedspread
Advanced sound/spelling links, including **ear** as
in clear, **ea** as in head and **silent letters** .

ecards

al
ounds
books.

How to use Book 2

The stories in Book 2 introduce your child to simple words including the short vowel sounds a as in cat, e as in hen and i as in pig.

- Read each story through to your child first. Having a feel for the rhythm, rhyme and meaning of the story will give him* confidence when he reads it for himself.

- Have fun talking about the sounds and pictures together. What repeated sound can your child hear in each story?

- Help your child break new words into separate sounds (eg. c-a-t) and blend them together to say the word.

- Point out how words with the same written ending sound the same. If h-en says 'hen', what does he think t-en or K-en might say?